Foreword

Minibeasts come in many thousands of different sorts, and millions of inc
Although they are small, these little creatures are very important. Some
good for plants, while others pollinate our fruit trees. Yet others help k
and pond waters clean, or provide food for larger animals, such as birds and mammals.
Only a few are bad for us, like those that bite and spread diseases, or destroy crops.

Many minibeasts clearly differ in how they look, as well as how they live. But some
that seem similar are actually very different, while others that look
totally different are really just the same. All very confusing. Because
of this, and because they are small and there are so many different
sorts, it can be hard to find out what they are. This wonderful little
book will help you get a real start in telling one minibeast from
another. Once you get started, you will probably want to know
more about their fascinating world. This book can help you do that
too. Good luck with your bug hunting, identifying - and studying!

Dick Vane-Wright
(Head of the Insect Department, at The Natural History Museum, London)

Male Stag Beetles

Contents

Wasp Spider

This key will help you to name all of the common types of minibeast that you encounter on your bug hunt.

Start at page 8, then follow the key to discover the identity of your creatures. Once you have named your minibeast turn to the back of the book where you can find out more about it.

Happy Hunting!

Green Shield Bug

Hummingbird Hawk moth

Minibeasts

Minibeasts are everywhere in the summer, they buzz around you in the garden, wander across paths when you are out walking and try to steal your food when you have a picnic. It is great fun to hunt for them and there are many different kinds of minibeast to find. This book should help you discover a little more about the minibeasts that you find and make your minibeast safaris even more fun.

The name *minibeasts* has been given to all small animals such as insects, snails, woodlice and worms (sometimes called creepy crawlies). Some of them have 6 or more legs whilst others like slugs, snails and worms have none.

Biodiversity

We think there are about 12.5 million different kinds of plants and animals on the planet but no one can be absolutely sure how many there are. We do know that out of this huge number about 8.9 million are minibeasts. This means that out of all the living things known to us, two thirds of them are minibeasts. This makes them one of the most important groups of living things on the planet. They also occur in huge numbers. It was once calculated that there are a thousand, million, billion insects (which are just one group of minibeasts) alive on the planet at any time.

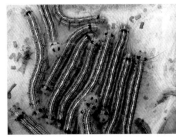
Lackey moth caterpillars

That is 20 million insects for every human alive and 10 billion insects for every square kilometre of dry land.

Most of this huge variety of minibeasts is found in tropical forests and grasslands, but there are still vast numbers that can be found in the British countryside.

The Key

The key has been written to help you identify the creatures that you find. It will not identify every minibeast you may come across as some of the rarer minibeasts have been left out in order to make the key easier to use. Once you have used the key to identify your minibeast turn to the back of the book if you would like to find out more about it.

Take care of your minibeasts

While minibeasts look very tough, if they are put back in the wrong place they can die very quickly. It is very important to return your minibeasts to the place they were found so that they will survive. When you are minibeast hunting don't forget to always put logs and stones back as you found them.

Classification

Each different kind of minibeast is known as a species. As there are about 8.9 million different minibeast species it can be difficult if you need to talk about just some of them. To overcome this problem they are divided into groups. For instance all those with six legs are in one group. Each of these groups is divided into smaller groups. Eight-legged minibeasts are divided into those with two body parts and those with one. These groups are then divided into smaller groups until you are left with a small group of species that are very similar to each other.

A small group of **Species** is known as a **Genus**. More than one genus is called a group of genera.

Genera that have many features in common are placed together in a group known as a **Family**.

Families that are similar to each other are grouped together and are known as **Orders**.

Groups of Orders are known as **Classes** and groups of Classes are called a **Phylum**.

Groups of Phyla are called **Kingdoms**.

This process of grouping together animals that are similar in some way is called classification.

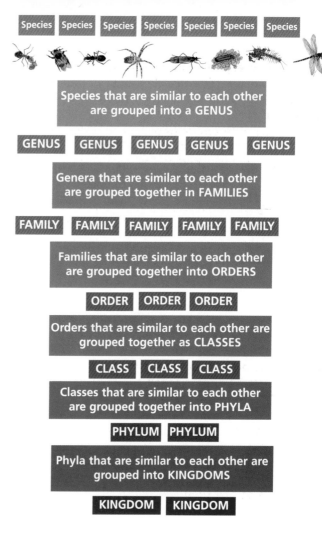

Species | Species | Species | Species | Species | Species | Species

Species that are similar to each other are grouped into a GENUS

GENUS | GENUS | GENUS | GENUS | GENUS

Genera that are similar to each other are grouped together in FAMILIES

FAMILY | FAMILY | FAMILY | FAMILY | FAMILY

Families that are similar to each other are grouped together into ORDERS

ORDER | ORDER | ORDER

Orders that are similar to each other are grouped together as CLASSES

CLASS | CLASS | CLASS

Classes that are similar to each other are grouped together into PHYLA

PHYLUM | PHYLUM

Phyla that are similar to each other are grouped into KINGDOMS

KINGDOM | KINGDOM

Moulting and Life Cycles

Many minibeasts have an external skeleton. This means that their skin acts like a suit of armour that protects their insides and supports their weight. This is very different from humans and other large animals who have an internal skeleton to support their body weight and a thin delicate, waterproof skin on the outside. As minibeasts feed and grow their bodies cannot increase in size because their rigid skin stops them. The only way they can become bigger is to grow a new skin under the old one, then crack open the old skin and climb out of it. This is known as moulting. As the new skin is soft at this time, the minibeast can blow itself up to its new size and wait for the new skin to dry and harden. The minibeast can continue to grow until it has filled its new skin, then it has to change its skin again.

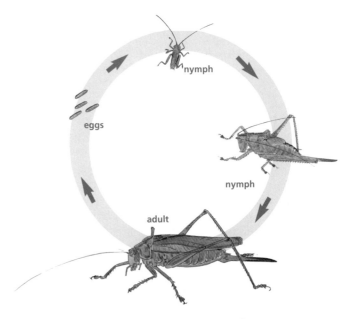

Insect life cycle without a pupal stage
Great Green Bush-cricket

Sea Slater shedding skin

Minibeasts that have an external skeleton can be divided into two groups, those that have a pupal stage and those that do not. Minibeasts that do not have a pupal stage emerge from their eggs looking like tiny versions of their parents. These miniature minibeasts are known as nymphs if they are insects and juveniles if they are not. They shed their skins a number of times as they grow before becoming an adult. If the adult has wings these will only appear in the last moult. Nearly all minibeasts have this sort of life cycle.

Minibeasts that have a pupal stage hatch from their eggs looking nothing like their parents. The young minibeast is known as a larva. The larva will grow and moult several times until it is ready to turn into an adult. It then produces a new skin underneath the old one and moults to become a pupa. This is a tough new skin that will protect the minibeast while it changes from a larva into an adult.

Small Tortoiseshells

This change is known as metamorphosis. Once the change is complete the pupal case will crack open and the adult will emerge.

People often wonder where all the minibeasts go during the winter. This is a bad time of year for them as there is little food available and it is often too cold for them to move around. Minibeasts have many ways of surviving the winter. Some adults lay their eggs in the autumn and then die leaving the next generation to spend the winter as eggs. Others that have a pupal stage in their life cycle spend the winter in a sheltered spot as pupae. Some, such as the Small Tortoiseshell butterfly, hibernate as adults. A few are active in the winter as they are able to survive and move around when it is cold.

Small Tortoiseshell hibernating in a shed

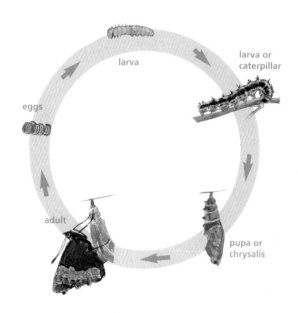

larva

larva or caterpillar

eggs

pupa or chrysalis

adult

Insect life cycle with a pupal stage
Small Tortoiseshell

5

Identifying the different parts of minibeasts

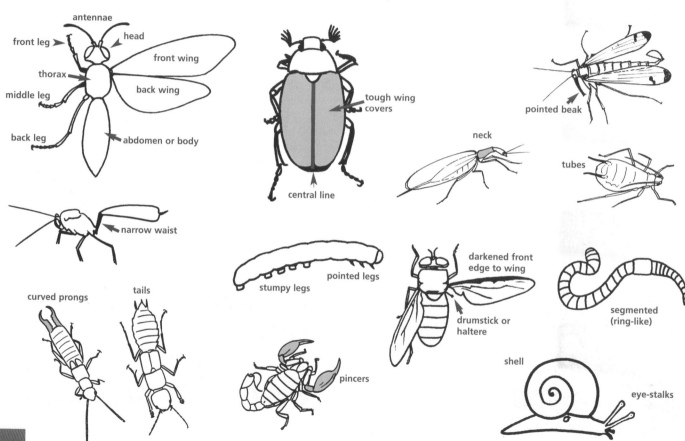

antennae
front leg
head
front wing
thorax
back wing
middle leg
back leg
abdomen or body

tough wing covers
central line

pointed beak

neck

tubes

narrow waist

pointed legs
stumpy legs

darkened front edge to wing
drumstick or haltere

segmented (ring-like)

curved prongs
tails

pincers

shell
eye-stalks

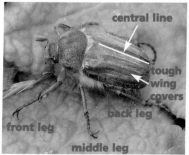

central line

tough wing covers

back leg

front leg

middle leg

Summer Chafer beetle

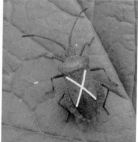

Squash bug

wing cases divided by an **X**

back leg

Dark Bush-cricket

Planthopper

wing cases divided by a **Y**

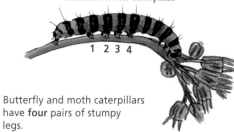

Cinnabar moth caterpillar

1 2 3 4

Butterfly and moth caterpillars have **four** pairs of stumpy legs.

Sawfly larvae have **six** or more pairs of stumpy legs.

1 2 3 4 5 6

Sawfly larva

antennae

eye

Hornet

Horntail

ovipositor (egg laying device)

Cranefly - showing 'drumsticks' or halteres

legs

Chafer beetle larva

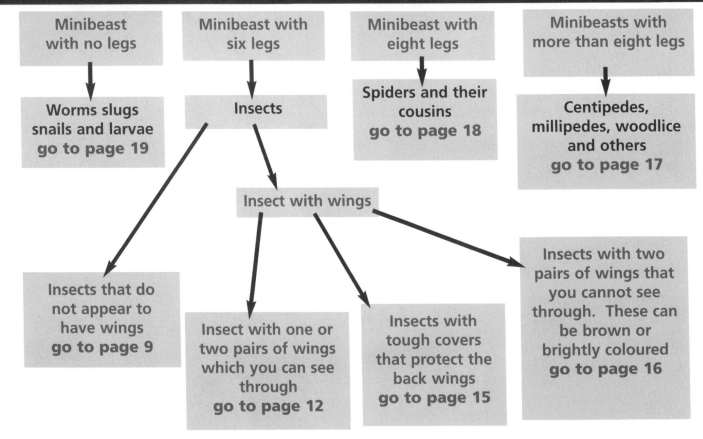

START HERE
How many legs does your minibeast have?

Minibeast with no legs

Minibeast with six legs

Minibeast with eight legs

Minibeasts with more than eight legs

Worms slugs snails and larvae
go to page 19

Insects

Spiders and their cousins
go to page 18

Centipedes, millipedes, woodlice and others
go to page 17

Insect with wings

Insects that do not appear to have wings
go to page 9

Insect with one or two pairs of wings which you can see through
go to page 12

Insects with tough covers that protect the back wings
go to page 15

Insects with two pairs of wings that you cannot see through. These can be brown or brightly coloured
go to page 16

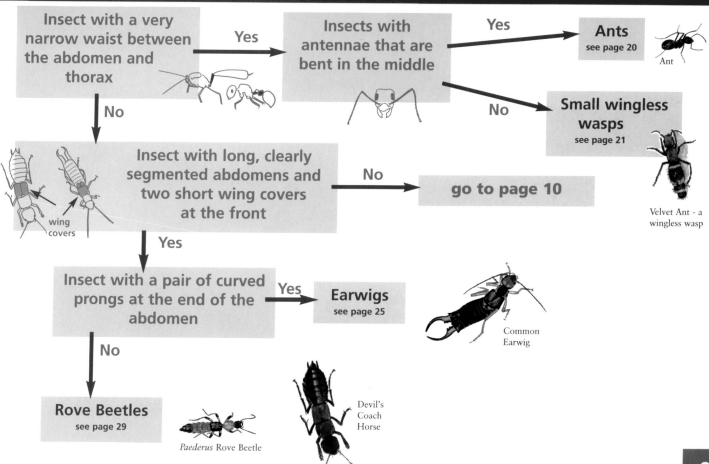

Insect with a very narrow waist between the abdomen and thorax

Yes → Insects with antennae that are bent in the middle

Yes → **Ants**
see page 20

Ant

No → **Small wingless wasps**
see page 21

Velvet Ant - a wingless wasp

No ↓

Insect with long, clearly segmented abdomens and two short wing covers at the front

wing covers

No → go to page 10

Yes ↓

Insect with a pair of curved prongs at the end of the abdomen

Yes → **Earwigs**
see page 25

Common Earwig

No ↓

Rove Beetles
see page 29

Paederus Rove Beetle

Devil's Coach Horse

9

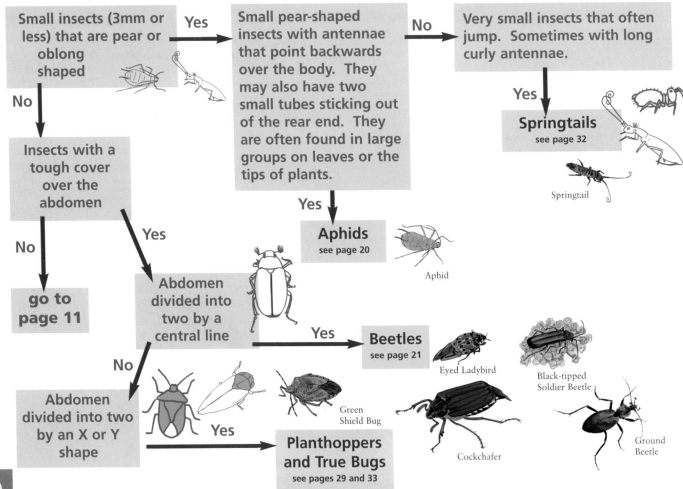

Small insects (3mm or less) that are pear or oblong shaped

Yes →

Small pear-shaped insects with antennae that point backwards over the body. They may also have two small tubes sticking out of the rear end. They are often found in large groups on leaves or the tips of plants.

No →

Very small insects that often jump. Sometimes with long curly antennae.

Yes
Springtails
see page 32

Springtail

No ↓

Insects with a tough cover over the abdomen

Yes ↓

No ↓

go to page 11

Abdomen divided into two by a central line

Yes

Aphids
see page 20

Aphid

Yes →

Beetles
see page 21

Eyed Ladybird

Black-tipped Soldier Beetle

No ↓

Abdomen divided into two by an X or Y shape

Green Shield Bug

Yes →

Planthoppers and True Bugs
see pages 29 and 33

Cockchafer

Ground Beetle

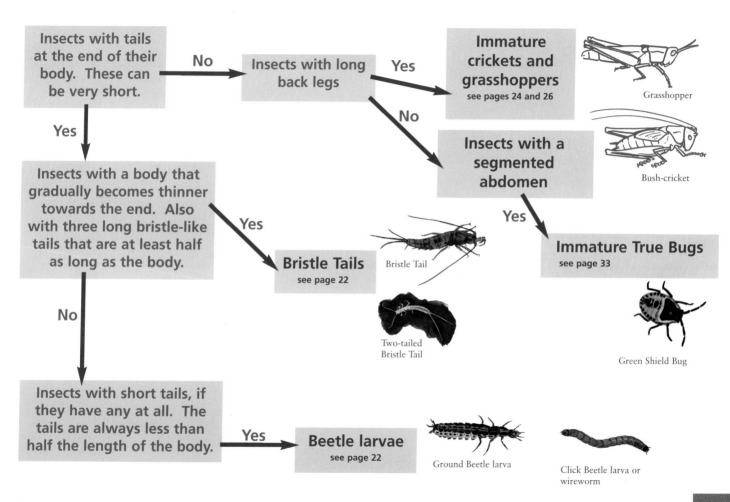

Insects with tails at the end of their body. These can be very short.

No → Insects with long back legs

Yes → **Immature crickets and grasshoppers**
see pages 24 and 26

Grasshopper

Bush-cricket

No → Insects with a segmented abdomen

Yes ↓

Insects with a body that gradually becomes thinner towards the end. Also with three long bristle-like tails that are at least half as long as the body.

Yes → **Bristle Tails**
see page 22

Bristle Tail

Two-tailed Bristle Tail

Yes → **Immature True Bugs**
see page 33

Green Shield Bug

No ↓

Insects with short tails, if they have any at all. The tails are always less than half the length of the body.

Yes → **Beetle larvae**
see page 22

Ground Beetle larva

Click Beetle larva or wireworm

START HERE
Insects with one or two pairs of
wings that you can see through

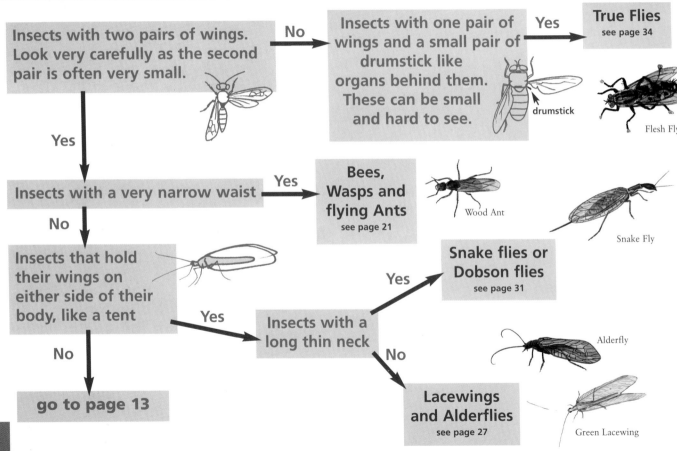

Insects with two pairs of wings. Look very carefully as the second pair is often very small.

No → Insects with one pair of wings and a small pair of drumstick like organs behind them. These can be small and hard to see.

drumstick

Yes → **True Flies** see page 34

Flesh Fly

Yes ↓

Insects with a very narrow waist **Yes** → **Bees, Wasps and flying Ants** see page 21

Wood Ant

No ↓

Insects that hold their wings on either side of their body, like a tent

Snake Fly

Yes → Insects with a long thin neck

Yes → **Snake flies or Dobson flies** see page 31

No → **Lacewings and Alderflies** see page 27

Alderfly

No ↓

go to page 13

Green Lacewing

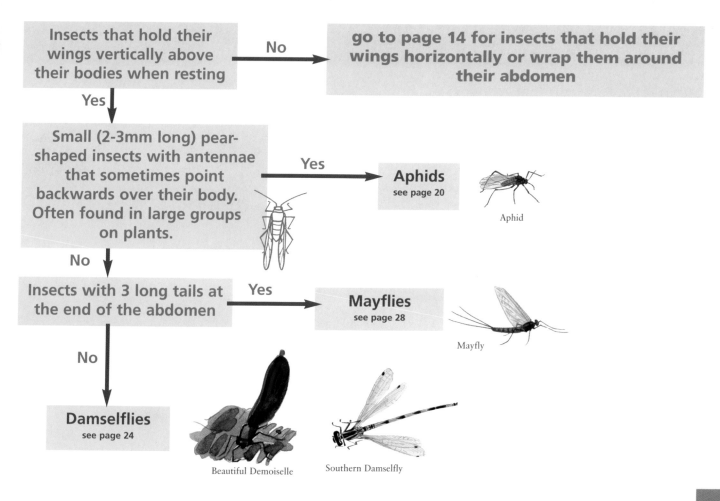

Insects that hold their wings vertically above their bodies when resting

No → go to page 14 for insects that hold their wings horizontally or wrap them around their abdomen

Yes ↓

Small (2-3mm long) pear-shaped insects with antennae that sometimes point backwards over their body. Often found in large groups on plants.

Yes → **Aphids** see page 20

Aphid

No ↓

Insects with 3 long tails at the end of the abdomen

Yes → **Mayflies** see page 28

Mayfly

No ↓

Damselflies see page 24

Beautiful Demoiselle

Southern Damselfly

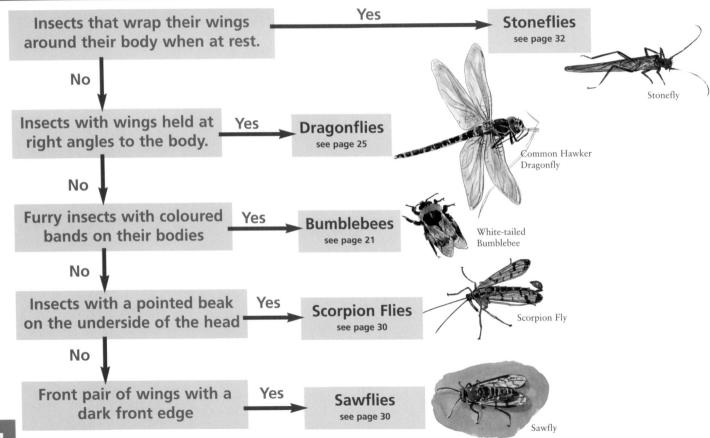

Insects that wrap their wings around their body when at rest.

Yes → **Stoneflies** see page 32

Stonefly

No ↓

Insects with wings held at right angles to the body.

Yes → **Dragonflies** see page 25

Common Hawker Dragonfly

No ↓

Furry insects with coloured bands on their bodies

Yes → **Bumblebees** see page 21

White-tailed Bumblebee

No ↓

Insects with a pointed beak on the underside of the head

Yes → **Scorpion Flies** see page 30

Scorpion Fly

No ↓

Front pair of wings with a dark front edge

Yes → **Sawflies** see page 30

Sawfly

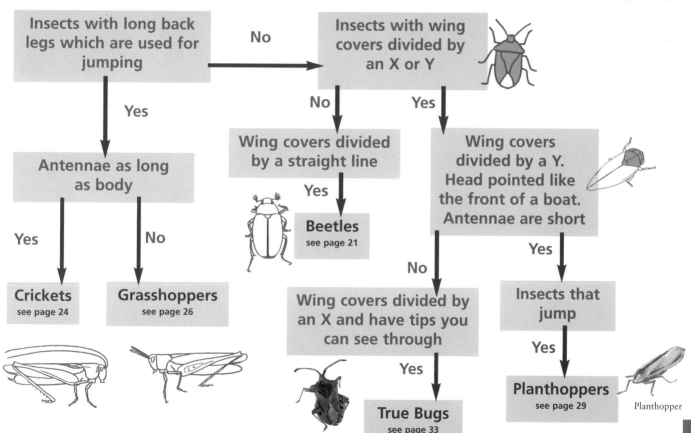

Insects with long back legs which are used for jumping

No → Insects with wing covers divided by an X or Y

Yes ↓

Antennae as long as body

Yes ↓ Crickets
see page 24

No ↓ Grasshoppers
see page 26

No ↓ Wing covers divided by a straight line

Yes ↓ **Beetles**
see page 21

Yes ↓ Wing covers divided by a Y. Head pointed like the front of a boat. Antennae are short

No ↓ Wing covers divided by an X and have tips you can see through

Yes ↓ **True Bugs**
see page 33

Squash Bug

Yes ↓ Insects that jump

Yes ↓ **Planthoppers**
see page 29

Planthopper

15

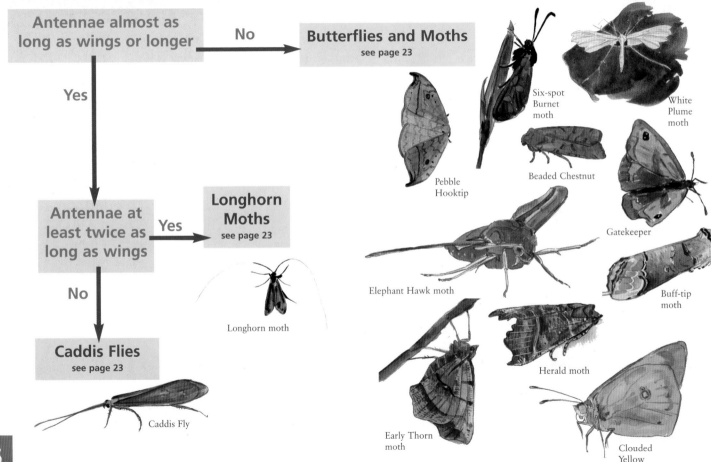

Antennae almost as long as wings or longer

No → **Butterflies and Moths** see page 23

Yes ↓

Antennae at least twice as long as wings

Yes → **Longhorn Moths** see page 23

No ↓

Caddis Flies see page 23

Longhorn moth

Caddis Fly

Six-spot Burnet moth

White Plume moth

Pebble Hooktip

Beaded Chestnut

Gatekeeper

Elephant Hawk moth

Buff-tip moth

Herald moth

Early Thorn moth

Clouded Yellow

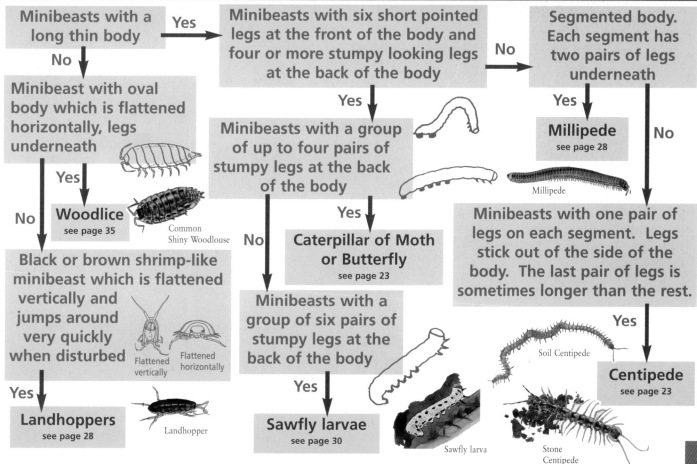

Minibeasts with a long thin body

Yes →

No ↓

Minibeast with oval body which is flattened horizontally, legs underneath

Yes ↓

No

Woodlice
see page 35

Common Shiny Woodlouse

Black or brown shrimp-like minibeast which is flattened vertically and jumps around very quickly when disturbed

Flattened vertically

Flattened horizontally

Yes ↓

Landhoppers
see page 28

Landhopper

Minibeasts with six short pointed legs at the front of the body and four or more stumpy looking legs at the back of the body

No →

Yes ↓

Minibeasts with a group of up to four pairs of stumpy legs at the back of the body

Yes ↓

No

Caterpillar of Moth or Butterfly
see page 23

Minibeasts with a group of six pairs of stumpy legs at the back of the body

Yes ↓

Sawfly larvae
see page 30

Sawfly larva

Segmented body. Each segment has two pairs of legs underneath

Yes ↓

No

Millipede
see page 28

Millipede

Minibeasts with one pair of legs on each segment. Legs stick out of the side of the body. The last pair of legs is sometimes longer than the rest.

Yes ↓

Soil Centipede

Centipede
see page 23

Stone Centipede

17

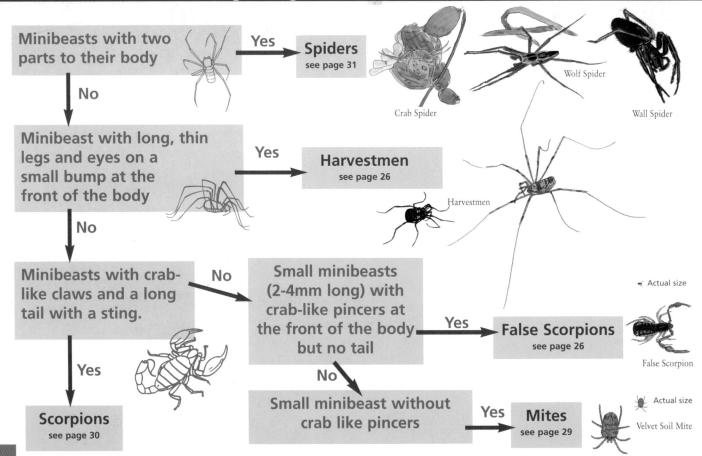

Minibeasts with two parts to their body — Yes → **Spiders** see page 31

Crab Spider

Wolf Spider

Wall Spider

No

Minibeast with long, thin legs and eyes on a small bump at the front of the body — Yes → **Harvestmen** see page 26

Harvestmen

No

Minibeasts with crab-like claws and a long tail with a sting. — No → **Small minibeasts (2-4mm long) with crab-like pincers at the front of the body but no tail** — Yes → **False Scorpions** see page 26

Yes ↓

Scorpions see page 30

No ↓

Small minibeast without crab like pincers — Yes → **Mites** see page 29

Actual size

False Scorpion

Actual size

Velvet Soil Mite

18

START HERE
For minibeasts without legs

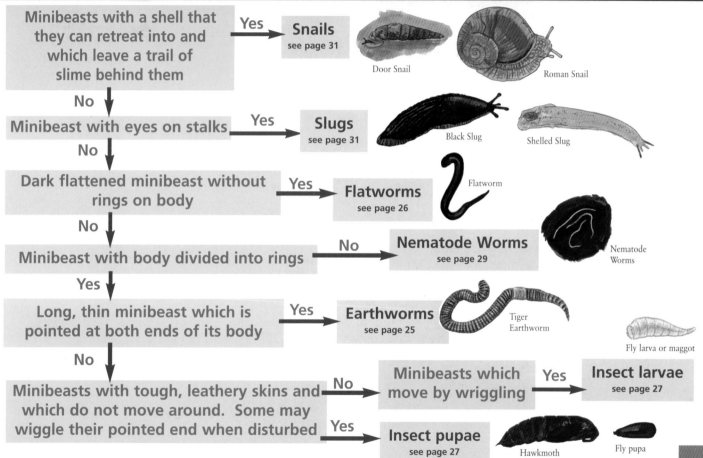

Minibeasts with a shell that they can retreat into and which leave a trail of slime behind them

Yes → **Snails** see page 31

Door Snail

Roman Snail

No ↓

Minibeast with eyes on stalks

Yes → **Slugs** see page 31

Black Slug

Shelled Slug

No ↓

Dark flattened minibeast without rings on body

Yes → **Flatworms** see page 26

Flatworm

No ↓

Minibeast with body divided into rings

No → **Nematode Worms** see page 29

Nematode Worms

Yes ↓

Long, thin minibeast which is pointed at both ends of its body

Yes → **Earthworms** see page 25

Tiger Earthworm

Fly larva or maggot

No ↓

Minibeasts with tough, leathery skins and which do not move around. Some may wiggle their pointed end when disturbed

No → Minibeasts which move by wriggling → **Yes** → **Insect larvae** see page 27

Yes → **Insect pupae** see page 27

Hawkmoth pupa

Fly pupa

19

Facts About Your Minibeasts

 Minibeasts that have an exoskeleton.

 Minibeasts with a pupal stage in their life cycle.

The Latin Name refers to the order see page 3.

Ants

Latin Name *Hymenoptera* (The ants are a Family within the *Hymenoptera* which are known as the *Formicidae*)

36 species in Britain

Red Wood Ant

Ants live in large colonies. For most of the year all the ants are female. In fact they are all sisters as they have hatched from eggs laid by the queen. Most British ants are predators, catching any small minibeasts that they encounter and taking them back to the nest to eat. Swarms of flying ants are a common sight in the

Red Wood Ants

summer. These are winged male ants and the new queens that have emerged from every nest in the neighbourhood at the same time. The males try to mate with the new queens but as there are many thousands of males and only a few queens most are unsuccessful. Once the queens have mated they fly to the ground, shed their wings and look for a good nest site in which to start a new colony. The males die within hours of leaving the nest.

Aphids or Greenfly

Latin Name *Homoptera*
500 species in Britain

Aphids feed on plant sap and are often found in large groups known as a colony. In the summer they are all females which give birth to live daughters. At this time of year they are wingless but will produce daughters with wings if the colony begins to run out of food. This allows the young aphids to fly to a new plant. Aphids spend the summer on one kind of plant then in the autumn they fly to a different type of plant on which they spend the winter.

winged aphid

aphid

Bees and Wasps

Latin Name *Hymenoptera*

6600 species in Britain

The largest member of this group is the hornet which can be over 2 cm long. Bees range from the large bumble bees to small solitary bees of 4 mm in length. There are also many very small wasps that can be less than 1 mm long. Many of these are parasites that lay their eggs in or on other insects. The eggs hatch and the larvae eat the insect alive. Others lay their eggs inside plants which cause strangely shaped swellings to grow around them which are known as galls. Many of the common bees and wasps live in colonies and are known as social insects. Only the queen lays eggs, which hatch out to become female workers. The workers feed the larvae, build and repair the nest. Social wasps feed on other minibeasts while social bees collect pollen and nectar.

White-tailed Bumblebee

Parasitic Wasp

Common Wasp

Beetles

Latin Name *Coleoptera*

3729 species in Britain

There are many different beetle lifestyles. Some are predators feeding on other insects, many more are plant feeders eating every part of a plant. Other foods eaten are dung, animal skins, wool, wood and dried foods such as flour or beans. Many beetles live almost all of their lives under water. A few live in the nests of other animals such as bees, birds and mice.

Great Diving Beetle

Dung Beetles

Dor Beetle

Black-tipped Soldier Beetle

Eyed Ladybird

Harlequin Beetle

Hazel Weevil

Bloody-nose Beetle

Beetle larvae
Latin Name *Coleoptera*

3729 species in Britain

Ground Beetle larva

Beetle larvae live in as many different situations as adult beetles. They feed on a wide range of foods, from dung to decaying plants. All parts of living plants are eaten and many eat dried plant material such as seeds. Many are predators eating other minibeasts.

Longhorn Beetle larva

Click Beetle larva

Summer Chafer larva

Bristletails

Latin Names *Thysanura* and *Diplura*

22 species in Britain

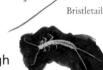
Bristletail

Bristletails can be found living on the seashore and rocks above the high tide line. They are also found in houses and they used to be common in bakeries. On the sea shore they feed on decaying plant material while in houses and bakeries they eat spilled foods and the paper packaging containing foods. Two-tailed Bristletails are often common in compost heaps.

Two-tailed Bristletail

Bumble Bees

Latin Name *Hymenoptera*
26 species in Britain
See Bees and Wasps on page 21.

Buff-tailed Bumble Bee

Butterflies and Moths
Latin Name *Lepidoptera*

**2500 species in Britain
(60 butterflies, 2440 moths)**

All the British butterflies fly in the day whilst most moths fly at night, but there are some moths that fly in the daytime. All the moth and butterfly caterpillars feed on plants. Some eat leaves whilst others eat stems. Some even live inside the plants that they are eating. Others eat dried plant materials such as birds nests or flour. Almost all the adult butterflies and moths feed on nectar which they drink from flowers through a long tongue called a proboscis. The proboscis is coiled under the head when not in use.

Painted Lady

Eyed Hawk moth

Six-spot
Burnet moth

Caddis Flies
Latin Name *Trichoptera*

199 species in Britain
152 have larvae which live in cases and
47 which do not live in cases

Caddis Fly

Caddis flies spend their larval life in ponds, lakes and rivers, from which they emerge as flying adults. These resemble some moths but have hairs rather than scales on their wings. Adults often emerge together in large numbers, forming dense swarms. The adults feed little or not at all. Most

are weak flyers and do not travel far from water, resting on the vegetation to mate. A few are stronger flyers and are attracted to house and street lights. Eggs are laid in the water or on bank side vegetation.

Caddis Fly

Centipedes
Latin name *Chilopoda*

41 species in Britain

Soil Centipede

These are predators that are found in dark and damp places, usually in leaf litter or soil, under stones or beneath the bark of logs and fallen trees. They have between 15 and 101 pairs of legs, depending on the species, with a single pair of legs on each segment. The centipedes with 15 pairs of legs can run very fast whilst those with more than 15 move more slowly. They have a pair of poisonous fangs under their heads, which they use to bite and paralyse their prey.

Stone Centipede

Crickets
Latin Name *Orthoptera*

16 species in Britain

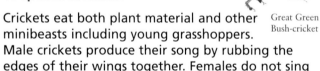
Great Green Bush-cricket

Crickets eat both plant material and other minibeasts including young grasshoppers. Male crickets produce their song by rubbing the edges of their wings together. Females do not sing at all. Some are large insects that can be up to 5 cm long.

Dark Bush-cricket

Wood Cricket

Damselflies
Latin Name *Odonata*

17 species in Britain

These are fragile looking insects that are always found close to water. Some have bright blue metallic wings whilst others have transparent wings. They lay their eggs attached to underwater plant stems and the young (known as nymphs) hatch and live under water where they feed on other small minibeasts. They take one year to reach their full size in southern Britain but two years in northern Britain, where the climate is colder and the nymphs grow more slowly. In the spring and summer, nymphs crawl up the stems of water plants where they shed their skins and emerge as adults. Adult damselflies are predators that catch their prey in flight.

Southern Damselfly

Beautiful Demoiselle

Red-eyed Damselfly

Dragonflies
Latin Name *Odonata*

30 species in Britain

Dragonflies are strong fliers that can move at high speeds and as a result they are often found a long way from water. They hunt on the wing catching smaller flying insects.

Common Hawker

Southern Hawker

Like their cousins the damselflies, their young live underwater feeding on other minibeasts. The dragonfly nymphs can take between two and six years before they are fully grown.

Earwigs
Latin Name *Dermaptera*

7 species in Britain

Earwigs are active at night and spend the day hiding in cracks and crevices in the soil, under stones and inside garden sheds and outbuildings. They feed on living plants and as most gardeners know, they have a particular liking for flower petals. Earwigs are unusual in that the female guards her eggs and looks after

Common Earwig and eggs

her young after they have hatched. She feeds and cares for them until they have shed their skins for the second time.

Lesne's Earwig

Earthworms
Latin Name *Oligochaeta*

44 species in Britain

Some earthworms live entirely underground whilst others live in leaf litter or under moss and stones. Others spend the day in the soil and move onto the surface at night to feed. All earthworms feed on plant material of one kind or another. They eat living plant roots and leaves as well as dead plant material. Those that live in the soil eat large amounts of soil and digest any plant material and small animals that are swallowed.

Tiger Earthworm

25

False Scorpions

◄ Actual size

Latin Name *Pseudoscorpiones*

26 species in Britain

False scorpions are predators that feed on other small minibeasts such as mites and springtails. Some false scorpions hunt their prey by walking around, whilst others sit and wait for the next meal to pass by. Many have a poison gland which produces a venom that paralyses the prey. False scorpions also produce silk which they use to construct a shelter in which to shed their old skins. They live in leaf litter, bird and mammal nests and under the bark of dead trees.

False Scorpion

False Scorpion

Flatworms

Latin Name *Turbellaria*

29 species in Britain (only 6 of these can be found in damp situations on land).

Terrestrial flatworms feed on other minibeasts that live in the soil such as slugs or earthworms. Two species have been accidentally introduced from Australia and New Zealand. These may become pests as they eat more earthworms than the British flatworms.

Flatworm

Grasshoppers

Latin Name *Orthoptera*

14 species in Britain

Grasshoppers feed mainly on grasses of various kinds. They sing by rubbing their back legs against the edge of the front wings. Males sing to attract females but female grasshoppers will also sing. Groundhoppers are smaller relatives of the grasshoppers which live on bare ground and damp mud.

Meadow Grasshopper

Cepero's Groundhopper

Harvestmen

Latin Name *Opiliones*

24 species in Britain

Most harvestmen are scavengers, which will feed on anything they come across in their travels. They will attack small insects or larger ones that are ill, damaged or dead, as well as eating vegetation. Some of our harvestmen specialise in eating snails.

Harvestmen

Insect larvae

The Latin name depends on which type of insect it is.

Insect larvae are usually very different from the adult insects that they will become. There

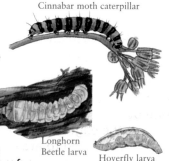

Cinnabar moth caterpillar

Longhorn Beetle larva

Hoverfly larva

are many different kinds of insect larvae. Even within a single insect group there can be vast differences in shape and size. They can range in appearance from thin worm-like larvae that live in the soil, to large fast-moving larvae with enormous jaws. The main task of a larva is to eat as much as it can in order to become as big as possible. The larger the larva the larger the adult will be, and a big adult is more likely to survive.

Orange-tip butterfly pupa

Insect pupae

These come in many shapes and sizes that range from a few millimetres long for some midges to giants of five centimetres for the big hawk moths. Some are

Fly pupa

Ground Beetle pupa

Hawk moth pupa

smooth cylindrical cases, rounded at both ends. Others display the shape of the wings and head of the insect that will hatch from it, these usually have a pointed end. Many of these can wiggle this pointed end when touched, in an effort to frighten other animals that may try to eat them.

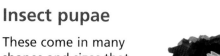

Lacewings and Alderflies

Latin Name Lacewings *Neuroptera*
Latin Name Alderflies *Megaloptera*

60 species in Britain

Lacewings are predators as both larvae and adults. The larvae are small maggot-like creatures that crawl over the vegetation in search of aphids to eat. Both larvae and adults feed by sucking their prey dry through their pointed but hollow jaws. The larvae of Alderflies live in ponds and streams so the adults are often found sitting on the vegetation nearby.

Green Lacewing

Alderfly

Giant Lacewing

Landhoppers
Latin Name *Amphipoda*

1 species in Britain
It comes from western Australia and is found in western Britain, South Wales and the Western Isles of Scotland.

Landhoppers feed on partially decomposed or rotting vegetation. They are related to the sandhoppers that can be found under seaweed on the beach. Landhoppers are usually found in woods amongst the leaf litter but also occur in gardens, garden centres and nurseries. When they occur in gardens they often come into houses by mistake. Land hoppers need dark damp conditions and cannot survive temperatures near to freezing.

Actual size

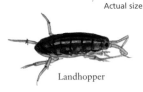

Landhopper

Mayflies
Latin Name *Ephemeroptera*

48 species in Britain

Mayfly

Adult mayflies live for a very short time varying from a single day to one week. Most young mayfly nymphs live on the bottoms of streams, rivers and ponds for one year but some take two years before they become adults. The nymphs feed on a mixture of plant debris and algae. All of the adults in a stretch of river or stream emerge at the same time forming a dense black cloud of insects that floats like smoke over the river. They mate in the air and the females drop their eggs into the water. The nymphs are very sensitive to chemical pollution and the presence or absence of mayflies in rivers can be used as an indication of water pollution.

Millipedes
Latin Name *Diplopoda*

53 species in Britain

Millipedes feed on live or decaying plant material. They are found in leaf litter, under bark, in the soil and sometimes in trees. Some have rounded bodies, whilst others have flat backs. The Pill Millipedes look like woodlice but have more than 14 legs. All millipedes have two pairs of legs on each segment of their body.

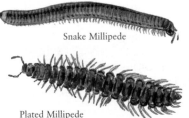

Snake Millipede

Plated Millipede

Pill Millipede (compare with Pill Woodlouse on page 35)

Mites
Latin Name *Acari*

1720 species in Britain

Actual Size

Velvet Soil Mite

Mites are very small, ranging in size from 2mm to less than a tenth of a millimetre. They can be found in almost every possible habitat from mountains and woodlands to the dust inside our houses. They also feed on a wide variety of things including living and dead plants, shed human skin, other mites and fungi. Some mites are parasites living amongst the fur and under the skin of mammals.

Nematode worms
Latin Name *Nematoda*
The number of species in Britain is at present unknown.
These worms are common in the soil where they can occur in huge numbers (5 million per cubic metre). Some feed on the bacteria or algae that exist in the water occurring between soil particles, while others feed on small soil-dwelling animals.

Nematode Worms

Planthoppers
Latin Name *Homoptera*

350 species in Britain

Planthopper

These have long pointed mouth parts which they use to pierce plants and suck out the sap. They can jump short distances to avoid predators.

Nymph of Planthopper in 'cuckoo spit'.

Rove beetles
Latin Name *Coleoptera* (*Staphylinidae*)

1000 species in Britain

Rove beetles are fierce predators which eat any minibeast smaller than themselves. They range in size from 1mm to 25mm in length. Many can fly and have a complicated method of folding their wings under the short wing covers. Some live inside ant nests where they feed on rubbish left by the ants or ant larvae.

Paederus Rove Beetle

Devil's Coach Horse

Devil's Coach Horse eating a ground beetle

Sawflies

Latin Name *Symphyta*

513 species in Britain

Adult sawflies feed on pollen whilst the larvae eat the stems or leaves of plants. They are called sawflies because the adult females of some species have an ovipositor on the end of their abdomen that looks like a wood saw. This is used to cut a slit in the stems of plants so that the female can lay her eggs inside.

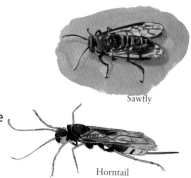
Sawfly

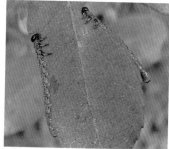
Horntail

Sawfly larvae

Scorpions

Latin Name *Scorpionidae*

1 species in Britain

Scorpions are predators that feed on other minibeasts, which they catch with their crablike claws. The sting is only used to subdue difficult prey. The European species that occurs in Britain is about 3cm long and is found in holes in walls where it spends most of its life. It is not dangerous to humans. They only leave the hole when they have grown too big for it or in the case of males to find a mate. Colonies have been found in old walls around London and south-east England, but individuals regularly turn up in imported goods at ports around the country.

Scorpion

Scorpion Flies

Latin Name *Mecoptera*

4 species in Britain

They feed mainly on the bodies of dead minibeasts but occasionally on live ones, decaying meat, over-ripe fruit and bird droppings. Females lay their eggs in the soil and the larvae move between the soil and the litter layer eating decaying plant and animal material.

Scorpion Fly

Slugs & Snails
Latin Name *Gastropoda*

94 land snail species and 29 slug species in Britain

These are plant eaters that only come out to feed at night. They use a small file-like tongue on the underside of their heads to scrape off the surface layers of the leaves, stems and even roots of most plants. Two species of British slug have a small shell. These slugs are also different in that they are carnivores that eat other minibeasts.

Roman Snail

Door Snail

Black Slug

Shelled Slug eating an earthworm

Snake flies or Dobson flies
Latin Name *Megaloptera*

4 species in Britain

Both adults and larvae are predators of smaller minibeasts. The larvae live under bark while the adults fly freely hunting for prey on trees and bushes. They use their long necks to strike at their prey.

Snake Fly

Spiders
Latin Name *Araneae*

647 species in Britain

All spiders are predators, feeding on other minibeasts including other spiders. They are well known for building the large round orb webs that are a common sight in gardens and the countryside.

These are not the only webs built by spiders. Some build funnel webs, some build sheet webs. Some do not build webs at all but hunt by sight. They walk around until they spot the next meal then slowly creep up on their prey until they are close enough to pounce. Others sit in one place and wait for their prey to pass by, then when it is close enough the spider will grab it with its long front legs.

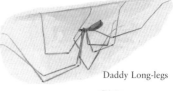
Daddy Long-legs

Orb-web Spider

Wall Spider

Woodlouse-eating Spider

Most spiders have a poisonous bite, which helps to stop their prey struggling when caught. All British spiders are harmless to humans. They feed by regurgitating digestive juices from their gut onto the prey and then suck the partially digested food back into their stomachs.

Crab Spider

Jumping Spider

Springtails
Latin Name *Collembola*

300 species in Britain

These are very small minibeasts that range in size from 4 mm down to 0.5 mm in length. They live in the soil or in leaf litter, although some live on the water surface of ponds and rock pools. They feed on partially decayed

Actual Size

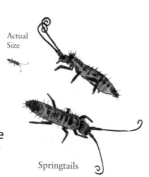
Springtails

vegetation. They are known as springtails because many of them have a short tail that is bent under the body and can be released like a spring, catapulting them into the air.

Stoneflies
Latin Name *Plecoptera*

33 species in Britain

Adult stoneflies are nearly always found on the stones or vegetation close to streams and rivers. The adults live for 2 to 3 weeks in which time most species do not feed at all, while some eat algae, which they scrape from stones and tree trunks. After mating the females lay their eggs on the water surface, where they sink to the stream bed. The nymphs hatch from the eggs and spend up to 3 years feeding and growing. Most nymphs eat algae and moss from the stream bed but a few are predators of other insect nymphs.

Stonefly

Stonefly

True Bugs

Latin Name *Heteroptera*

516 species in Britain

All the true bugs have piercing mouth parts that are used to suck fluids from either plants or animals. Many feed on plants, sucking sap from the stems or leaves. Others prey on other minibeasts, injecting saliva into their prey, which partially digests their insides making it easier to suck their bodies dry.

Most live on dry land but a few live on the surface of ponds (pond skaters) and a few live underwater (water boatmen).

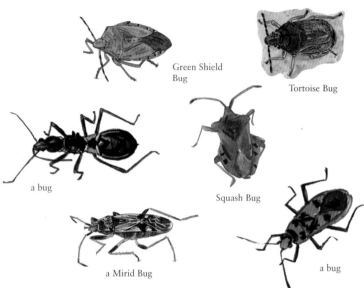

Green Shield Bug

Tortoise Bug

a bug

Squash Bug

a Mirid Bug

a bug

shieldbugs

Meadow Plant Bug

a shieldbug

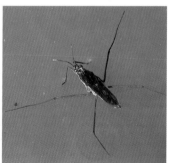

a pond skater

True flies

Latin Name *Diptera*

6000 species in Britain

Flies range in size from a few millimetres to over 2 cm in length. They feed on just about everything, from dung to blood and from nectar to compost. Some are skilled fliers being able to stop and fly backwards whilst others just drift on the wind. A number of flies have larvae that live in fresh water. A few live on the seashore feeding on decaying seaweed, but most fly larvae live on dry land.

Flesh Fly

Hornet Robber Fly

Dance Fly

Crane Fly

St Mark's Fly

Twin-lobed Deerfly

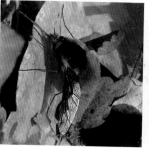
Dark-edged Bee-fly

Marmalade Hoverfly

Greenbottle

Woodlice

Latin Name *Isopoda*

48 species in Britain

These minibeasts live in dark and damp situations where they feed on dead plant material, leaves and wood. An important part of their diet is the mould and bacteria that grows on the decaying vegetation. Woodlice often eat the dung of other woodlice, as by passing the food through their gut twice they can extract more nutrients from the food. Some species are only found on the coast whilst others are found living in ant nests. All British woodlice have 14 legs.

Common Shiny Woodlouse

Pill Woodlouse

Common Rough Woodlouse

Sea Slater

Ant-nest Woodlouse

Pill Woodlouse

Great books to find out even more about minibeasts

Ugly Bugs. A Horrible Science Book
Nick Arnold. Published by Scholastic Children's Books.
Lots of fun and minibeast facts with great cartoons.

Minibeast Magic
Roma Oxford. Published by the Yorkshire Wildlife Trust.
Shows you loads of different ways to
catch your minibeasts using household materials.

If you want to get really serious try:

The Natural History of Insects
Rod & Ken Preston-Maffham.
Published by The Crowood Press.
Lots of excellent photographs and up-to-date science.

Key to Terrestrial Invertebrates
Steve Tilling.
Published by The Field Studies Council.
An identification key to all the orders of all the major
groups of minibeast found in Britain. You will need a
microscope to use this key properly.

Field Guide to Insects of Britain and Northern Europe
Michael Chinery.
Harper Collins.
A comprehensive introduction to all the insect orders of the
region, including keys to level of family. There are also
colour plates depicting a few representatives of each family.

Collins Guide to Insects of Britain and Western Europe
Michael Chinery
Harper Collins.
An introduction to the insect orders found in the region. Less
text than the previous volume but many more colour
illustrations which depict the common and distinctive insects.

The Bug Club
This club is open to children 'of all ages' - they produce 6
magazines a year and organise trips of interest to bug
hunters. More details at www.amentsoc.org or write to The
AES, PO Box 8774, London SW7 5ZG enclosing a stamped,
addressed envelope.

Acknowledegments

We would like to thank Martin Attrill, Dave Bilton, Brian and
Lorraine Bewsher, Karen Gresty, Sally Howell,
Chantelle Jay, Ivor Kenny, Darren Mann,
Geoff and Roma Oxford, Gordon Ramel,
Helen Read, Kevin Solman, Peter Sutton,
Joyce and Barnaby Walters for their very
helpful and enthusiastic comments on
the various drafts of this key. Dick Vane-
Wright for his foreword and valuable
comments. Jane Lamerton, for steering us
towards a text style that was minibeast
hunter friendly. Roger Mann, Robin Hibdige
and Colin Markham at Wotton Printers for their
help during the production of this booklet.

Orange-tip